DISNEY
PRINCESS

D1352237

Aurora

The Perfect Party

First published by Parragon in 2012
Parragon
Queen Street House
4 Queen Street
Bath BA1 1HE, UK
www.parragon.com

Copyright © 2012 Disney Enterprises, Inc.

Written by: Wendy Loggiar   Illustrated by: Studio IBOIX and Gabriella Matta
Edited by: Gemma Louise Lowe   Designed by: Joe Scott
Production by: Sarah Brown

ISBN 978-1-4454-4077-4
Printed in China

Aurora
The Perfect Party

This book belongs to:

Ella-Jo Walker

Chapter One

$\mathcal{P}$rincess Aurora opened her violet eyes. Sunlight was streaming through her bedroom window.

"Another beautiful day," she said with a smile, stretching her arms over her head. She had just had the most delightful dream that she was back living in the woodcutter's cottage with the three good fairies: Flora, Fauna and Merryweather.

For sixteen years, Aurora had lived in the forest with the fairies. She didn't know that she was a princess or that she was being hidden from the evil fairy, Maleficent. The good fairies had named her Briar Rose and had pretended to be her aunts. She lived with them in the Woodcutter's Cottage and she had a wonderful, happy childhood.

Even though Aurora had been living in her real home, the palace, for a year, she was still adjusting. She hopped out of bed and walked over to the window. Her husband, Prince Phillip, was outside feeding his horse a carrot.

The princess pushed the window open.

"Good morning!" she called, waving.

The prince turned. "Good morning, sleepy-head!" he said, looking up with a smile. "I'm just about to take Samson for a ride. Would you like to join me?"

Aurora thought for a minute. It would be fun to go for a morning horseback ride with Phillip, but her dream had made her eager to see the fairies.

"Maybe next time!" she said. "Have fun!"

The prince waved, then climbed onto Samson and trotted off.

Aurora opened her wardrobe and looked through her rail of beautiful gowns; they lay before her eyes in all the colours of the rainbow.

"Princess Aurora?" One of the palace servants knocked softly on her bedroom door. "The cook has made some delicious blueberry pancakes for you. Of course, there are also scrambled eggs, if you'd rather have those, or if you'd prefer, a big bowl of strawberries and whipped cream?"

"Oh, the cook is too kind. I certainly won't go hungry," Aurora laughed, "I'll be down in just a moment." Aurora reached for a long, flowing pink gown and her favourite pair of shoes, dressed quickly and hurried down the hallway.

The castle was the biggest and most beautiful place that Aurora had ever seen. It seemed as though each stairway and each closed door led to a new room. She still hadn't had the chance to see everything!

"Hello! Good morning." Aurora greeted the servants who were bustling to and fro. There were cooking staff, cleaning staff and gardening staff and even staff to polish the royal jewels! It took a lot of people to keep the castle in tip-top shape.

"You look as pretty as a daisy!" Flora said. She floated down the hallway towards Aurora with Fauna and Merryweather at her side.

When Aurora and Phillip had married, the three fairies had moved into the castle too. They had an entire wing just to themselves!

"Why, thank you!" Aurora smiled and twirled around. "Can you join me for breakfast?"

"Let's check our calendar," Fauna said. She pulled out her magic wand and *poof!* a calendar hovered in the air in front of them.

"It looks like we're available," Flora said. Fauna was just about to zap the calendar away when Merryweather stopped her.

"Wait just a minute! Do you realize what date is coming up?" Merryweather looked at the three puzzled faces. "It's almost exactly one year since the day that we all moved into the castle together!"

"A whole year," Fauna said, sighing happily.

"My! How time flies," said Flora, shaking

her head. "It seems like only yesterday that we were all living in the woodcutter's cottage."

"I dreamed about the cottage last night!" Aurora exclaimed. "You all took such good care of me there. I can never thank you enough for all that you did."

"We loved every minute of it, my dear," Merryweather replied.

"Every second," Fauna added.

"Every… every… every moment," Flora declared. "Sometimes I wish we could all go back there to live together again."

The fairies chattered on about their favourite memories from the cottage as they entered the royal dining room with Aurora. Suddenly, the princess had an idea.

I'm going to throw the fairies a grand

surprise-party to celebrate our first year together in the castle, she thought with excitement. Aurora knew that the palace staff would be busy planning her own birthday party, which was just over a week away, but she would throw the surprise-party for the fairies a couple of days before. It would be the biggest and grandest celebration that the castle had ever seen!

Chapter Two

$\mathscr{A}$fter breakfast, the fairies all left together, which gave Aurora time to plan. She went into her bedroom and pulled out a pink journal and a plumed blue quill from her desk.

"Now, what kind of party would they like best?" she said aloud, tapping her chin with the quill.

Outside of her door, she heard the fairies'

voices. As Aurora walked quietly down the hall, the sounds grew louder. Flora, Fauna and Merryweather were outside on one of the castle terraces.

Aurora tip-toed silently past the large glass doors which opened onto the terrace and hid behind a long velvet curtain, clutching her journal tightly.

"Ahh, yes. That looks just splendid," Fauna said. She was arranging a gigantic bouquet of flowers in a crystal vase. The vase hovered in the air – the fairies didn't like to do *anything* without magic! Fauna snipped off a few of the leaves and adjusted some of the petals. Then she stepped back to get a full view of her creation.

"If only I had some forget-me-nots."

"Are those the pink and blue flowers that you used to pick?" Flora asked from the other side of the terrace. She was flitting around, so that she could monitor the watering cans that she'd enchanted as they swept over the flowerpots, pouring just the right amount of water into them.

"Yes. They're my absolute favourite flowers," Fauna replied.

"You know, you could always turn those roses into forget-me-nots," Merryweather said, eyeing Fauna's wand as the blue fairy was busily untangling the strings of some wind chimes.

Fauna sighed. "That's not the same. They never smell as fragrant. The best ones in the whole world grow in a flower bed near the

woodcutter's cottage." She shook her head. "There are some things that even magic can't do."

Smiling to herself, Aurora opened up her journal and wrote:

Forget-me-nots (pink and blue) for Fauna.

Then she continued to listen to the fairies from behind the curtain.

"I do know what you mean, Fauna," Merryweather said. "I love my bedroom here at the castle, of course – it couldn't be any nicer – but there was a group of songbirds who had a nest near my room in the cottage. Waking up to that concert every morning was one of my favourite things. I miss it terribly!"

Aurora wrote in her book again:

A chorus of songbirds for Merryweather.

"And while we're at it, let's not forget all the sweet red strawberries Briar Rose – I mean, Aurora – used to gather on her walks," Flora said, nodding. "They were so juicy and delicious!"

Aurora wrote a third note:

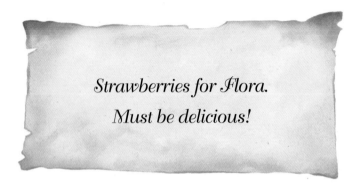

Strawberries for Flora.
Must be delicious!

The princess looked over her list. That's it! she thought. We'll have a grand party made up of the simple things we all miss from our time in the forest. She smiled, delighted with her idea.

Aurora turned and walked back down the hallway before the fairies could discover her.

She paused outside the royal ballroom. This was one of her favourite places in the castle. She and Phillip had held several parties there for their friends.

Aurora stepped inside the empty ballroom. Heavy crystal chandeliers hung from the ceiling, and mirrors and tapestries lined the walls. She looked down at her notebook – flowers, birds and strawberries. It was funny how the simplest of things could make the fairies so happy. She imagined how the elegant room would look with a chorus of songbirds and vases filled with forget-me-nots. This party would certainly be an unexpected change from the usual palace parties!

"Aurora? Is that you?" Prince Phillip poked his head inside the ballroom's grand doorway. "What are you doing in here all by yourself?"

"Planning the most perfect party in

the world!" she exclaimed. She ran over to the prince and gave him a hug, laughing as he twirled her around. The princess told Phillip about her idea.

"Won't it be a wonderful surprise for the fairies?"

Phillip scratched his head. "Strawberries and birds?" he asked. "That sounds so... well, it sounds lovely!"

Aurora smiled. "I knew you would agree!" she said. "I'm going to need your help," she continued.

The prince knelt down on one knee and waved his arm with a royal flourish.

"At your service, m'lady. Your wish is my command."

Aurora giggled. "Then please, darling, stand up. We haven't got a moment to waste!"

Chapter Three

"What do you think of this one?" Aurora asked. She had a floppy orange hat on her head. Then she pulled it off and put on a straw hat with long pink ribbons that tied under her chin. "Or is this better?"

Aurora and Phillip were upstairs in the castle. The prince was sitting on a cushioned bench, watching as Aurora tried on a range of hats and wigs. He looked very bored and a

little confused. "I'm still trying to figure out what exactly is going on," he said.

The princess took a calm and deep breath. "This party has to remain a secret. It will be unlike any event the fairies or the castle have ever seen."

"There have been a lot of events here," the prince reminded her. "We've had every theme imaginable – masked balls, holiday dances, birthday teas…."

Aurora's eyes were shining. "I know! That's exactly my point. This will be a completely different kind of party. Something that will remind the fairies of the time when we all lived together in the forest." She gave Phillip a kiss on the cheek. "The fairies are so dear, and they've done so much for me and my family. But we did have such fun when I was a little girl." She remembered blowing bubbles as they did the dishes and dancing with a broom when it was time to clean.

Phillip thought for a minute. "Could one of the servants go instead?"

The princess had considered that, but since everyone was busy planning for *her* birthday party, she wanted to do as much of the work for this party as she possibly could herself. "I know right where the flowers are and the strawberries. Plus, I really want this to be a gift from me."

"Well, what if I go with you?" Phillip suggested.

Aurora shook her head. "It will take some time to gather everything," she said. "If we're both gone for that long, the fairies will suspect something."

The prince nodded. "I'll keep the fairies distracted. Do you think you can finish in time?"

Aurora bit her lip. "I hope so. The party will be held four days from now. I'll have three days to find what I need and then, on the last day, we can decorate."

"Now," she said, turning back to the pile of hats, "it's time to find something completely unprincess-like!"

Chapter Four

Later that day, while the fairies were taking their afternoon nap, Aurora snuck out of the castle. She looked down at her simple lavender and white dress. She had decided on a white hat with a purple bow and her long blonde hair was tucked up underneath it. On her arm, she carried a basket to fill with flowers and berries.

Aurora smiled as she hurried away from

the castle. She thought she looked just like any other subject in the kingdom. She turned down a narrow wooded path that was lined on either side with tall trees and ferns.

The woodcutter's cottage was a fair distance from the castle. After walking for some time, Aurora stepped into a sunny clearing and sighed with happiness.

"The cottage!" she exclaimed.

Her old home looked just as she remembered it – the thatched roof, the small windows, the winding walk that led to the front door. It did seem a little smaller now that she had become used to living in a castle, but it was every bit as dear to her as it had always been.

Joyfully, Aurora began to sing and within

a few moments, her voice had drawn some woodland animals.

"Why, you recognize me, don't you?" she said, as two chirping bluebirds landed on a nearby tree branch.

Two fluffy-tailed squirrels stood holding acorns. Three small chipmunks had stopped chasing each other to listen to her sing and a group of cottontail rabbits gathered at her feet.

"I've missed you all so much," the princess said, smiling at her old friends.

Suddenly, the sound of approaching hoofbeats startled Aurora – someone was coming her way!

"Oh!" Aurora cried with a gasp. She hastily adjusted her hat.

A cart came into view, carrying a farmer and his family. They pulled to a stop beside the cottage.

"Good day, madam," the farmer said as he tipped his hat to Aurora. "Could you tell us which road leads back to the village? We seem to have taken a wrong turn somewhere."

Aurora smiled. She gave the farmer directions. "When you see the castle turrets over the hill, you'll know that you're almost there," she said.

"Thank you, dear," the farmer's wife said. "We've been going in circles for an hour! You've been so kind to help. Won't you please take some berries?"

Aurora kindly accepted a basket of plump blackberries. "Thank you," she said and popped a berry into her mouth. "Mmm, these are delicious!"

The farmer and his wife thanked Aurora again and then they set off on their way.

Aurora turned back to her animal friends.

"Well, clearly my disguise worked!" she exclaimed. She told the animals all about the surprise party that she was planning for the fairies. "Will you help me? You're all invited to the big event, of course!"

The animals chirped, chattered and hopped. "I'll take that as a yes!" Aurora said happily.

A shadow passed overhead, and the princess looked up at the sky. The sun was starting to set.

"My goodness! I must be on my way!" If she didn't leave now, it would be dark by the time she returned to the castle.

"And I haven't even crossed one item off my party list!" she said, sighing. "Oh, well. At least the guests have been invited!"

Chapter Five

*F*auna, Flora and Merryweather were pacing up and down in the main hall of the castle. When they saw Aurora coming down the staircase, they fluttered to her side. She'd snuck back into the castle and quickly changed into her pink gown.

"Princess Aurora! Where have you been?" Fauna asked.

"We were beginning to worry about you,"

Flora said, throwing her arms around the princess in a tight hug.

Merryweather nodded. "We woke up from our naps and the prince told us you were in the stables. When we couldn't find you there, he said you might be in the kitchen. Then he thought that perhaps you'd gone for a walk in the garden."

Just then, Prince Phillip walked into the room, grinning.

"Ah, you've found her! I should have thought to check the main hall."

Aurora tried not to laugh. The prince was doing a great job of distracting the fairies. She couldn't wait to tell him how well her disguise had worked. Planning a surprise party was turning out to be a lot of fun!

The next morning, Aurora put on another simple dress, this time she decided on a blue one. She tied her long blonde hair back with a scarf.

"Remember, you must keep the fairies distracted again," she told the prince. They were behind the royal stables, hiding from the palace attendants.

"I've got it all covered," he said. "Last night, I told the fairies how much I loved that cake they made for my birthday and asked if they could make it again today."

Aurora frowned. "But that won't take them long at all!"

"It will if they can't find their wands," the prince said. He pulled three wands from his scabbard.

"That's absolutely...perfect!" Aurora exclaimed. The fairies would be shocked when they woke up to find that their wands were missing. For a moment she felt bad about upsetting them, but then she thought about the party she had planned for them, and how it would all be worth it.

The prince kissed her cheek. "Now, go!"

When Aurora arrived at the cottage, she set off down a worn footpath that led to Fauna's favourite flower bed which wasn't far from the cottage's front door. She carried a basket in the crook of her arm.

The sweet smell of the flowers told Aurora she was almost there. "Fauna was right," she said as she came to a large bed of pink and blue forget-me-nots. "Not even magic could create something as beautiful as this!"

She knelt down and took out a pair of garden shears that she had carried in her basket. Then she carefully began to cut enough flowers to make one of the biggest bouquets Fauna had ever seen.

When Aurora has finished, she hurried back to the castle. Phillip had found a couple of large vases for her and filled them with water. Aurora arranged the bouquet and hid it behind one of the long drapes in her room.

She took out her pink journal and put a big tick next to:

✓ *Forget-me-nots (pink and blue)*
for Fauna.

Then she changed into another gown and went downstairs.

The fairies were in the kitchen. Fauna

had frosting on her hat, Flora's cheeks were covered in icing and Merryweather had dough on her face.

"My, my, it smells delicious in here," Aurora said. "What's the occasion?"

"The prince asked us to make him a special cake," Fauna explained.

"And you decided not to use magic. How wonderful!" Aurora said. She dipped her finger in the frosting for a taste.

"Yes, well, we, um, decided it would be more special that way," Merryweather said as Flora backed her up with an anxious nod.

"I'm sure he'll appreciate it so much," Aurora told them. Then she left the fairies to their baking. Her plan was working out perfectly!

Chapter Six

*L*ater that night, Aurora found Prince Phillip tip-toeing out of the fairies' wing of the castle.

"I put their wands on Merryweather's bookshelf," the prince whispered. "I'm afraid they were worried about losing them."

"The poor dears," Aurora felt terrible, but she was almost done planning the party and the fairies still had no idea that she'd been sneaking out of the palace.

Aurora set off on another trip that

morning. She wore a straw hat and a bright red dress that she thought was the same colour as the strawberries she was going to collect for Flora.

Along the way, Aurora took a wrong turn. The sun was high in the sky by the time she had realized her mistake and she had to double back. She was very tired and a little frustrated, but the thought of Flora's delight over eating the most delicious strawberries in the forest again kept her motivated.

When at last she had found the old spot, she discovered that the berries weren't ripe enough yet.

"Oh, no!" she cried. "What am I going to bring Flora now?"

Suddenly, a robin flew over and landed

on Aurora's shoulder. She quickly explained that she was looking for: "The sweetest strawberries ever to be had!" The robin tweeted and flew further down the path. Aurora hurried to keep up.

When at last the robin stopped, Aurora clapped with delight. "Oh, thank you!" she said as she looked at row after row of bright red wild strawberries.

She popped one of the strawberries into her mouth. "Delicious!" she said. "These are exactly what Flora was talking about!"

Aurora filled her basket to the top. Then she pulled out her journal and looked at the note.

"I think I've found the yummiest berries in the kingdom!" she exclaimed, ticking it off her list.

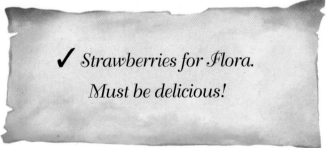

✔ *Strawberries for Flora.*
Must be delicious!

"Now, just one more thing," she said.
The robin was still chirping sweetly.

The robin couldn't help her pick berries, but he could help Aurora with a different task. She described her last item and the robin flew off. He returned a few minutes later with a bluebird and some other friends. Tweeting and singing, the birds made the most wonderful chorus that Aurora had ever heard.

"You must come tomorrow night and sing for Merryweather," she said. "Please, say you will."

The birds tweeted happily.

"Oh, thank you," Aurora said. "You've done so much for me already. Do you think you could do one more thing for me?"

The birds chirped.

"Wonderful." She leaned forwards and said, "Could you deliver a message to the castle for me?"

The birds chirped louder.

"Thank you all so much!" Aurora said. She carefully tore a piece of paper from her journal and wrote a note, she folded it in half and handed it to the robin. "Please make sure this goes to Claude, the butler."

The robin flew off with the scrap of paper tucked firmly in his beak.

Aurora looked at the last item on her list.

She smiled as she placed a third and final tick beside it.

✔ *A chorus of songbirds for Merryweather.*

Chapter Seven

*B*ack at the castle, Aurora spread a linen napkin over the basket of strawberries. Then she pushed it into the back of the pantry, where it was cool.

"There," Aurora said. She knew that after baking a cake without wands, the fairies were unlikely to return anytime soon, so there was no danger of them seeing the strawberries in the pantry.

The biggest delivery of party supplies

was yet to come. Aurora had arranged for the items to be hidden in the stables until the next morning. Everything had all come together perfectly!

Aurora changed out of her red dress into a pretty purple gown. She ran downstairs and out onto the back lawn, where she spotted a green blur, a blue blur and a red blur. The three fairies were on their hands and knees searching through the grass. "Flora? Fauna? Merryweather? What's going on?"

"Oh, princess, hello!" Flora said, jumping up. Her skirt was covered in clover and her cheeks were as pink as her dress. "Prince Phillip had the most terrible luck. He–"

"He lost a rare jewel this morning!" Fauna

interrupted. "It fell out of his pocket while he was riding Samson! We've been looking for it for hours."

"Oh, my goodness," Aurora exclaimed. Phillip must be frantic, she thought. Then she spotted him walking across the lawn towards them.

"Phillip! I've just heard what happened," she said, running to him. To her surprise, he gave her a wink. Suddenly, she realized, this was another distraction for the fairies!

"And wouldn't you know, the jewel has a spell on it. It can't be found by magic," Merryweather said huffily.

The prince held out his hand. Sitting in his palm was a glittering emerald-coloured gem.

"It turns out that I didn't drop it after all,"

he told them, wearing a sheepish grin. "It was in my pocket all along."

"In your pocket all along?" Flora repeated wearily.

"Isn't that wonderful," Fauna said, yawning. Her hat had slipped down to one side of her head, but she smiled.

Merryweather grunted. "Next time, perhaps Your Highness might check his pockets more thoroughly before sending us on a wild-goose chase."

"Merryweather!" Fauna whispered, giving the fairy a nudge.

But Phillip nodded. "I don't blame Merryweather for feeling frustrated. And I am so sorry to have troubled you. Why don't you all go inside and rest?"

Aurora agreed. "I'll have the cook make you your favourite dinner."

"That sounds lovely," Flora said gratefully.

The fairies slowly flew back to the castle.

"Keeping the party a secret hasn't been easy," Prince Phillip told Aurora as soon as the fairies were out of earshot.

"Only one more time to distract the dears – tomorrow morning," Aurora told him happily. "I need to make sure that they're far away from the royal ballroom so that we can set everything up for their party." She reached for his hand and they walked towards the castle. "Now the fun really begins!"

Chapter Eight

"*H*mmm, let's see. How about there?" Aurora pointed across the ballroom. "Right underneath that big crystal chandelier."

"As you wish, Your Highness," said a palace servant. He and another servant had moved the dining table all the way from the woodcutter's cottage into the centre of the room. It looked small and rustic in the elegant ballroom. Aurora beamed with pride as more servants carried in the cottage's chairs and another group balanced the cottage's dishes on large silver trays. The day of the party had finally arrived and now, her vision for the grandest celebration the castle had ever seen was coming to life!

The message she'd given to the birds in the forest was for a carriage to be sent to the cottage. The servants had loaded the dining furniture and other items onto it and snuck them into the castle.

"That's where our guests of honour will sit," Aurora told the servants as they arranged the chairs.

She picked up a familiar pink teacup and smiled. She knew the fairies would be thrilled to see these items from their old life.

The princess supervised and hummed a pretty tune as workers decorated columns with intertwining ivy garlands. Then she helped to make sure that the beautiful vases of forget-me-nots were placed throughout the room.

Claude the butler, hurried over to talk with Aurora. He was very eager to make sure the day was perfect. "Is everything as you wish, princess?"

"Oh, yes," Aurora told him, her eyes shining. "The fairies will love it!"

"We have even found a band of local musicians to play for us," Claude said. He pointed to the band members, who were setting up their instruments.

"Wonderful! The fairies love to sing

and dance," Aurora told him. Then she giggled as she watched the palace staff place simple tablecloths and hand-painted wooden candlesticks on the tables. The items from the cottage were certainly entirely different to the usual table settings that were used to the royal family!

A young woman, a new member of palace staff, shyly came over to Aurora. "Your Highness?" She gave a low curtsey. "I found this in the upstairs hall. I believe that it is yours?"

Aurora's eyes widened as the servant handed her the journal. All her notes for the party were in there!

"Oh, dear me," she said. "I must have dropped it on my way to breakfast this morning. I don't know what I would have done if the fairies had stumbled upon it. Our party could have been ruined!" She gave the young woman a grateful smile. "Thank you so very much."

Aurora clutched the journal to her chest. What if the fairies had seen it? Had her surprise been spoilt? She took a deep breath. The only thing to do was to keep preparing for the party.

Claude suddenly started waving his hands in the air, trying to get everyone's attention. "*S'il vous plaît!* Quiet, everyone! Shhh! I have just received word that the fairies are coming down the hallway right now. We must be as quiet as mice. We don't want them to know that we're in here."

A hush fell over the grand ballroom and Aurora's heart leaped into her throat. The fairies couldn't walk in now. The royal party guests hadn't even arrived yet! After all the hard work she, Prince Phillip and the palace staff had done, was the surprise about to be spoiled?

Chapter Nine

*E*veryone in the royal ballroom stopped what they were doing. Aurora's heart was racing. All her planning, all the flowers and strawberries and the songbird concert...the surprise couldn't be ruined now! After what seemed like forever, she heard a loud voice from behind the oak doors.

"Flora, Fauna, Merryweather! Please, wait!"

Aurora gasped. It was Prince Phillip!

"Yes, Your Highness?" the fairies said.

"There's a frog in the back garden who says that you have enchanted him. He's quite unhappy and he, uh, he wants to return to normal."

"I haven't enchanted any frogs lately," Fauna said. "Have you, Merryweather?"

"Not all month," the fairy replied.

There was a loud sigh from Flora. "I did turn a pesky rabbit into a frog last week. He just wouldn't stop eating my lilies and I couldn't stand it any longer. It served him right. It did."

The prince cleared his throat. "Well, the frog that was once a rabbit is asking to be turned back to his normal state. He seems rather finicky. Please, come and see him?"

It seemed that everyone in the ballroom was holding their breath as they waited to hear the fairies' reply.

A moment later, Aurora and the staff heard the fairies' shoes clicking along the hallway floor – they were going to see the frog.

The servants exchanged glances of relief and got back to work. The party would still be a surprise after all!

Aurora checked the clock. It was almost time for the guests to arrive. She tip-toed upstairs to her room to get dressed for the party.

She pulled her favourite pink gown out of her wardrobe. She'd thought for a moment about wearing one of her simple peasant dresses to the party, but she'd settled on the traditional gown instead. There would be plenty of royal guests as well as her forest friends.

After quickly brushing her long, blonde hair, Aurora hurried back to the ballroom. Guests from far and wide were beginning to arrive. Aurora hugged her parents and Phillip's father, King Hubert.

"What a fine party this is going to be," King Stefan said proudly as servants carried tray after tray of pies, frosted cakes and iced cookies into the ballroom. He kissed his daughter's head. "Lovely job, my dear."

The queen nodded. "Yes, darling. What a perfect party! I couldn't think of anyone more deserving than our dear fairies."

Aurora tried to stay calm. She walked over to the doorway to greet the guests as they arrived.

"Hello," Aurora said to a group of elegant ladies. "I'm so pleased you could be here." They looked beautiful in their gowns and jewels.

Then she heard some very non-royal sounds.

Squawk.

Chip-chip-chip.

Tweet.

"You're here!" Aurora cried. Her friends from the woods – the bluebirds, cardinals, chickadees, rabbits, chipmunks, squirrels and owl – flew into the ballroom. She looked kindly at the birds. "You know what to do, right?"

They tweeted back.

Aurora clasped her hands together. "Perfect!"

Then Claude hurried over to her. "It's time, princess. Are you ready?"

Aurora drew in a big breath. "I'm ready."

The room hushed. The lights dimmed and then the heavy oak doors swung open.

The fairies came fluttering into the ballroom in the middle of a conversation.

"I should have left him as a frog," Flora was saying. "He was such a pushy fellow–"

"Surprise!" cried all the guests, rising to

their feet and clapping loudly.

The fairies stopped. Their mouths dropped open.

Aurora gave the signal, and in an instant, all the candles in the room lit up. The windows swung open, letting in the summer breeze and the birds began singing the sweetest song in the world.

"Surprise, my dears!" Aurora cried happily. "Surprise, surprise!"

Chapter Ten

"*I* still can't believe you planned all of this for us," Merryweather said, shaking her head. She gazed around the room. "The decorations, the food, the guests – why, it's all so amazing!"

"We didn't suspect a thing, dearie!" Fauna said merrily.

"This is the biggest surprise of our lives," Flora added.

Princess Aurora was sitting at the fairies' table in the centre of the ballroom. The

party was in full swing. The fairies had been shown to their special seats as the band struck up a tune. Servants brought the fairies all sorts of treats served on their old cottage dishes.

Fauna pressed her face into the bouquet on the table and inhaled deeply. "These are the sweetest-smelling forget-me-nots I've ever sniffed," she said.

"And the strawberries are just as I remember them," Flora said, dipping a big red one into a bowl of whipped cream. "No, wait. They're better!"

The songbirds finished serenading a delighted Merryweather. The fairy wagged a finger at the princess.

"Very tricky you were, sending us on all

those wild-goose chases."

Aurora gave an innocent shrug. "If I hadn't, I would never have been able to give you the party you deserve, but I can't take all the credit," Aurora said as Prince Phillip walked over to their table. "I didn't know my husband was so good at keeping secrets!"

The prince winked at the fairies. "I'm so sorry I had to distract you so, will you forgive me?"

The fairies exchanged glances. At first they looked serious...but then they broke into happy smiles. "We do!" they said in unison.

"Then I hope you will honour me with a dance," he said, extending his hand to Fauna.

"Ooh! I'd love to," Fauna said. She took the prince's arm. As the band struck up their next song, Phillip and Fauna began to dance.

"My, he's so handsome," Flora said dreamily, leaning her chin on her hand. "Oops!" Her elbow knocked into her glass of fruit punch, toppling it over on the tablecloth. "Fiddlesticks," she said, dabbing the mess with some napkins.

"Here you go," Merryweather said, pulling out her wand. She zapped the tablecloth dry, changing it to blue in the process.

"Thank you," Flora said. She pulled out her own wand. *Zap!* The tablecloth was purple.

"Oh, you dears," Aurora said, laughing. "Don't you know that you aren't supposed to lift a wand at your own party?" She looked at them, her eyes dancing. "But I do think yellow would look absolutely perfect."

Zap! Suddenly the tablecloth was yellow. A startled Flora, Merryweather and Aurora looked up to see Fauna waving her wand.

"There we go!" she said breathlessly, tucking the wand back in her pocket. "Yellow it is." She plopped into a chair next to the princess and picked up her teacup. "I haven't danced like that in ages!"

"And I can see you haven't lost your touch," Aurora told her, patting her shoulder.

Just then, Prince Phillip came over to the table and bowed. "I've come to request the pleasure of another dance partner. Aurora, will you dance with me?"

Aurora turned to the fairies. "You don't mind, do you? Just for one dance?"

The fairies shook their heads. "Of course not," Merryweather replied. "Besides, it will give us some time to plan."

"Plan? Why, what do you mean?" Aurora asked, curious.

The fairies smiled. "Why, your birthday party, of course!" Flora said. "Only a few more days…."

The fairies winked. Aurora knew they would do something special. Just as she had for them.

"Now, shoo!" Merryweather said, waving the couple off. "We've got things to discuss."

Laughing, the prince and princess waltzed onto the dance floor as Flora, Fauna,

Merryweather and the rest of the guests clapped to the beat. A pair of rabbits danced beside them as the owl swooped overhead.

"This has been the best year of my life!" Princess Aurora said happily. "I can't wait to see what happens next!"

*Don't miss any of the
Disney Princess tales!*

Jasmine
The Missing Coin

*A*laddin's birthday is just around the corner. Jasmine wants to find him the perfect gift, so she sets off on the Magic Carpet with Rajah, the tiger. She is determined to track down a camel coin that Aladdin needs for his rare-coin collection. It's smooth sailing until the Magic Carpet suddenly stops, stranding Jasmine and Rajah in the desert! Will they find the special coin and make it back to the palace in time for Aladdin's birthday celebration?

Tiana
The Grand Opening

*T*iana has always dreamed of having her own restaurant and now her dream is about to come true! The grand opening is just around the corner, and all of Tiana's friends and family will be there, along with a famous food critic! Suddenly everything starts to go wrong! Her band-leader Louis loses his prized trumpet and then the power goes out after the guests arrive. Will the princess be able to fix things in time or will her big night be a royal disaster?

Cinderella
The Great Mouse Mistake

Cinderella's mouse friend Gus gives her a pretty bouquet of roses. Unfortunately, Cinderella gets in big trouble because he has picked the flowers from Lady Tremaine's garden! Cinderella takes Gus into town to replace the rosebush but she doesn't realize that it's the day of the village fair. In all of the excitement, Gus accidentally knocks over the giant cake made for the royal family! Luckily, Jaq, Luke, Perla and the rest of the mice join in to help bake a delicious new dessert. But will it taste as good as it looks?

Belle
The Mysterious Message

*I*t isn't easy being the prisoner of the Beast, but Belle is making the most of it. There are so many rooms to explore in the elaborate castle – including an amazing library. Things become even more interesting when Belle discovers a secret message hidden in one of the books. She soon realizes she's hot on the trail of a decades-old mystery! Will Belle, along with the help of Lumiere the enchanted candelabrum and a teacup named Chip, be able to solve this beastly case?

Ariel
The Birthday Suprise

Ariel's sister Adella is having a birthday celebration. It's going to be a fun-filled day complete with a birthday concert and Ariel is excited about visiting her family. Her only wish is that Prince Eric could go too. At the party, Adella wishes that Ariel could stay. That very moment, a rare solar eclipse hits and Adella's wish comes true! Will Ariel ever be able to break the spell and return to Eric and her life as a human?

Rapunzel
Tangled

Rapunzel has been locked in a tower
for her whole life. She decides that her
eighteenth birthday is going to be different,
she is going to see the floating lights that
appear in the sky, in person.

The opportunity arises when Flynn Rider
stumbles in through the tower window.
With Flynn as her guide on her hair-larious
adventure, will Rapunzel achieve her dream?
Will she discover her true identity?

Belle
Beauty and the Beast

Belle is an intelligent and beautiful young woman. She is very different from everyone else in her village and loves to read!

When her father is imprisoned by the fearsome Beast, Belle trades her freedom for her father's. What will Belle's life be like now she lives with the Beast in an enchanted castle? Will the Beast learn to love and be loved in return in time to break the enchantment on the castle?

The Little Mermaid

Ariel is a mermaid who longs to be part of the human world. When a storm wrecks Prince Eric's ship, Ariel saves his life and falls in love with him.

Enraged, her father bans her from contact with humans, so Ariel makes a deal with the sea witch, Ursula, to become human for three days. Will Ariel get True Love's Kiss from Eric before sunset on the third day? Will Ariel ever achieve her dream and become part of the human world?